Chester, the out-of-work dog

Author: Singer, Marilyn.
Reading Level: 3.4
Point Value: 0.5
ACCELERATED READER QUIZ# 6058

ROBERT E. LEE ELEMENTARY
ROUTE 8

D1479483

Chester

the
Out-of-Work
Dog

To Lenny, Nancy, and Alex
—M. S.

To Sue and Danielle
—C. B. S.

Thanks to Steve Aronson, Brenda Bowen, and,
especially, Maryann Leffingwell and Nola Thacker
—M. S.

Henry Holt and Company, LLC, *Publishers since 1866,* 115 West 18th Street, New York, New York 10011

Henry Holt is a registered trademark of Henry Holt and Company, LLC

Text copyright © 1992 by Marilyn Singer
Illustrations copyright © 1992 by Cat Bowman Smith
All rights reserved.
Published in Canada by Fitzhenry & Whiteside Ltd., 195 Allstate Parkway, Markham, Ontario L3R 4T8.

Library of Congress Cataloging-in-Publication Data
Singer, Marilyn. Chester the out-of-work dog / Marilyn Singer; illustrated by Cat Bowman Smith.
Summary: Chester's attempts to find a herding job after his human family moves into town
prove disastrous until he meets a group of lost children.
[1. Dogs—Fiction. 2. Work—Fiction.] I. Smith, Cat Bowman, ill. II. Title. PZ7.S6172Ci 1992 [E]—dc20 92-1141

ISBN 0-8050-5339-5
First published in hardcover in 1992 by Henry Holt and Company
First Owlet paperback edition—1997
Designed by Anna DiVito
Printed in the United States of America on acid-free paper. ∞

3 5 7 9 10 8 6 4

ROBERT E. LEE ELEMENTARY
ROUTE 5

Chester
the
Out-of-Work Dog

Marilyn Singer   Illustrated by Cat Bowman Smith

Henry Holt and Company • New York

There were two things Chester loved most
in the world—his family and his sheep.

Chester's family was named Wippenhooper. There was Ma
Wippenhooper, Pa Wippenhooper, and their children, Claude,
Maude, and Willy. The Wippenhoopers all looked different.

The sheep all looked pretty much the same. But Chester
could recognize each and every one. He had to. It was his job.

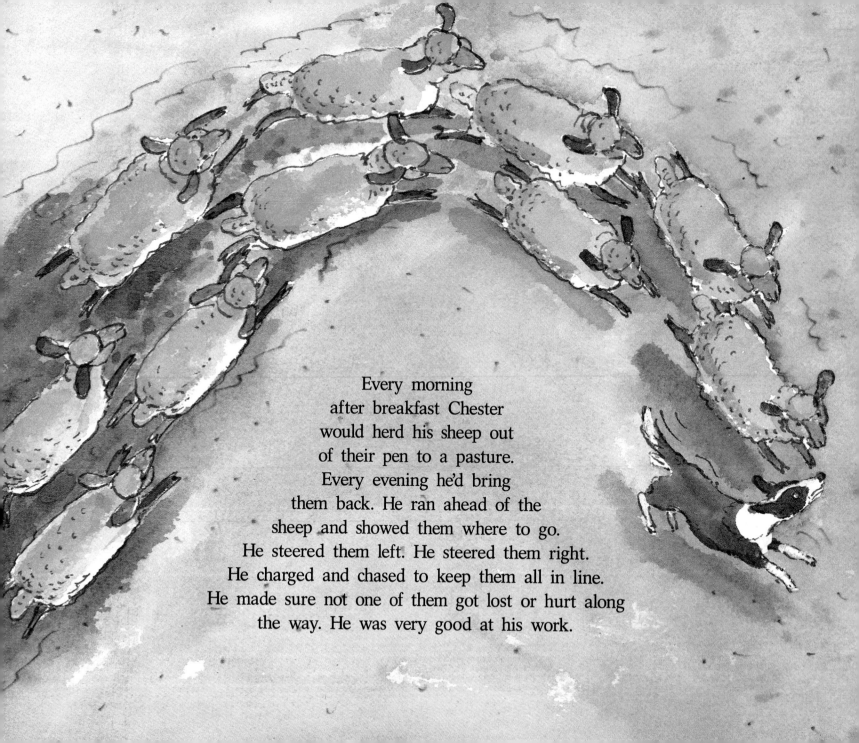

Every morning
after breakfast Chester
would herd his sheep out
of their pen to a pasture.
Every evening he'd bring
them back. He ran ahead of the
sheep and showed them where to go.
He steered them left. He steered them right.
He charged and chased to keep them all in line.
He made sure not one of them got lost or hurt along
the way. He was very good at his work.

At night when his work was done, Chester would settle
down happily with the Wippenhoopers first to listen to a little
television and later to the quieter country sounds of the wind
in the apple trees, the crickets in the grass, and the distant bleat
of his sleepy sheep. Then, curled up on Willy's bed, Chester
too would fall asleep and dream nothing but pleasant dreams.

But one day the Wippenhoopers sold the farm. They packed their belongings into a big truck and moved to town. Chester went with them. His sheep stayed behind.

That night after TV in their new apartment, Chester tried
hard to hear the wind and the crickets and most of all his sheep.
But what he heard instead was the screech of sirens, the blast of
car horns, and the sound of two cats fighting in an alley. And
when he fell asleep at last, curled up on Willy's bed, his dreams
were not pleasant at all.

In the morning Chester woke up early, ready as ever to go
to work. Then he remembered—he didn't have any work to do.
Neither did the Wippenhoopers. They all decided to take
Chester for a walk. They strolled by shops and houses. They
ambled past a precinct and a playground and then a public
school. "Look, Chester," said Maude. "This school has your
name. *Chester* A. Arthur Elementary School. Claude and I
will be going there. Isn't that great?"

Chester did not think it was great. His paws hurt too much from the concrete. His ears hurt from the noise. And he missed his sheep more than before.

A whole week went by. Pa Wippenhooper started a new job. Ma Wippenhooper fixed up the new apartment. Willy played with his old toys. Claude and Maude went to their new school.

Only Chester had nothing to do. Oh, he walked Claude and Maude to Chester A. Arthur Elementary School every day, but it wasn't enough. He was restless. He was bored. He needed to work. He needed to herd. So he decided if he couldn't herd his sheep, he'd just have to herd something else.

On Monday he herded a squirrel into a mailbox. On Tuesday he herded a pair of pigeons into the post office.

On Wednesday he drove three men and a refrigerator into a bowling alley. "Oh, dear," said Ma Wippenhooper, who had to apologize.

On Thursday he chased four garbage collectors with four large sacks of garbage into the fanciest restaurant in town. "Oh, Chester!" yelled Maude and Claude, dragging him out of the place.

On Friday he forced five firemen into a fountain.

On Saturday he sent six large policemen onto a statue of
George Washington's horse.

George Washington

But on Sunday in the park when he herded an entire girls'
softball team into the boys' bathroom, Pa Wippenhooper
shouted, "That's it! That's enough!" He snapped on Chester's
leash and scolded him all the way back to the apartment.

"What are we going to do with him?" Ma Wippenhooper sighed over dinner that night. She looked at Chester and shook her head. Claude and Maude looked at him too and frowned. Even Willy wouldn't give him a pat.

Chester lowered his head. His ears and tail drooped. He slunk under the kitchen table and stayed there all night. He did not go to sleep on Willy's bed. He did not go to sleep at all. It was clear to him his family didn't need him anymore. But perhaps his sheep still did. So, just as the sun was coming up, before the Wippenhoopers rose, he quietly climbed out the window and set out for his old home.

He trotted purposefully past the shops
and the houses, the precinct, the playground,
and Chester A. Arthur Elementary School.

A man tried to pet him.

Another tossed him a stick.

An old woman offered him a biscuit.

A newspaper girl tried to take him home.

But he kept on going and going. For miles he walked
until he reached a field near the edge of town.

Suddenly he stopped and stared and stared some more. Sheep! What Chester was staring at were sheep. Ten of them in all, with curly coats and twitching tails. But they didn't look quite like his sheep. For one thing, they were all standing on their hind legs.

He moved in closer and sniffed the air. They didn't smell like his sheep either. And when he moved closer still and heard their voices, he knew they weren't sheep at all. They were kids!

"What are we going to do?" one of them cried.
"We've been lost for a whole hour and now the
bus won't start. We'll never get there. We'll be the only
school in the county that won't be performing at the festival."

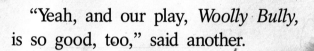

"Yeah, and our play, *Woolly Bully*,
is so good, too," said another.

"We'll have to walk,"
suggested a third.

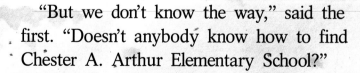

"But we don't know the way," said the
first. "Doesn't anybody know how to find
Chester A. Arthur Elementary School?"

Chester's ears pricked up. His tail began to wag. He reached
the children in two big bounds. "I do!" he shouted, though what
they heard was "Woof!" And then he began to herd them
on their way.

He ran ahead of the kids and showed them where to go. He steered them left. He steered them right. Through the field and back to town, he charged and he chased to keep them all in line. He made sure not one of them got lost or hurt along the way. And soon he brought them, giggling and cheering, straight up the steps of the school.

The principal was waiting at the door. When the children
told her what Chester had done, she invited him to come in and
see their play. Chester was delighted. He sat in the auditorium
between Claude and Maude, who were overjoyed that he had
returned, and watched the play. And though he didn't understand
it at all, he still had a good time.

The other Wippenhoopers were very proud when they learned what he had done. So was Chester.

The next day he was prouder still when he started his brand-new job—a school-crossing guard. He knew without a doubt he'd be very good at his work.